The New York Times Best-Selling Series by
Henry Winkler & Lin Oliver

Here's HANK

You Can't Drink a Meatball Through a Straw

ILLUSTRATED BY SCOTT GARRETT

Grosset & Dunlap
An Imprint of Penguin Random House

To Jamie Gangel—a stand-up friend!—HW

To Paula and Mark Waxman with a W and much love—LO

For the Furmstons, Mark, Michelle,
Betty, Daisy, and Ren—SG

GROSSET & DUNLAP
Penguin Young Readers Group
An Imprint of Penguin Random House LLC

Text copyright © 2016 by Henry Winkler and Lin Oliver
Productions, Inc. Illustrations copyright © 2016 by Scott Garrett.
All rights reserved. Published by Grosset & Dunlap, an imprint of
Penguin Random House LLC, 345 Hudson Street, New York,
New York 10014. GROSSET & DUNLAP is a trademark of
Penguin Random House LLC. Printed in the USA.

Typeset in Dyslexie Font B.V.
Dyslexie Font B.V. was designed by Christian Boer.

Library of Congress Cataloging-in-Publication Data is available.

ISBN 978-0-448-48658-1 (pbk)   10 9 8 7 6 5 4 3 2 1
ISBN 978-0-448-48659-8 (hc)   10 9 8 7 6 5 4 3 2 1

The books in the Here's Hank series are designed using the font Dyslexie. A Dutch graphic designer and dyslexic, Christian Boer, developed the font specifically for dyslexic readers. It's designed to make letters more distinct from one another and to keep them tied down, so to speak, so that the readers are less likely to flip them in their minds. The letters in the font are also spaced wide apart to make reading them easier.

Dyslexie has characteristics that make it easier for people with dyslexia to distinguish (and not jumble, invert, or flip) individual letters, such as: heavier bottoms (b, d), larger than normal openings (c, e), and longer ascenders and descenders (f, h, p).

This fun-looking font will help all kids—not just those who are dyslexic—read faster, more easily, and with fewer errors. If you want to know more about the Dyslexie font, please visit the site www.dyslexiefont.com.

CHAPTER 1

"Oh boy! Oh boy! Oh boy!"
I yelled at the top of my lungs.
"The pizza's here!"

"How do you know?" my best
friend Frankie Townsend asked.
"I didn't hear the doorbell ring."

"My nose knows," I told him.
"I can sniff out pepperoni a mile
away."

It was Friday pizza night.
Frankie and my other best friend,
Ashley Wong, and I were sitting
in my living room playing this card

game we made up called Florida Coconuts. I'd explain the rules to you, but they don't make any sense, even to us. It involves dropping a deck of cards on the loser's head, instead of a real coconut, which would leave a lump.

I got up and ran to the front door. Our dog, Cheerio, followed me. He can sniff out pepperoni a mile away, too. I taught him that. My mom was there balancing a huge pizza box in her hands. My younger sister, Emily, was next to her, holding a paper bag that smelled like Italian salad and garlic rolls. Standing next to her was a tall girl wearing a white chef's hat.

"Mom, I've never been so glad

to see you in my whole life!"
I said. "Emily, I'm not that happy
to see you. And you with the
crazy hat, I have no idea who
you are."

"Hank," my mom said, coming
into our apartment. "This is your
cousin Judith Ann. Remember,
I told you she was coming in from
Chicago to spend the weekend
with us. We're hosting her while
her parents are away at a business
conference."

"Whoops," I answered. "That must have slipped right through my brain and out my left ear. Or maybe it was my right ear. But who cares when there's pizza involved?"

I reached out and took the box from my mom's hands and headed for the dining-room table.

My dad brought plates and a big roll of paper towels from the kitchen. It was going to be our usual Friday pizza feast and movie night.

"Dig in, Judith Ann," I called to her. "Take off your crazy hat and grab a slice while it's hot."

Judith Ann walked over to the dining-room table and stared at our pizza.

"No thanks," she said. "I don't eat that type of pizza."

"Oh," my dad said. "Are you allergic to wheat?"

"No," Judith Ann said. "But I only like pizza I make myself, with goat cheese and artichokes."

"Judith Ann is quite an excellent cook," my mom explained. "In fact, in case you have forgotten," she said, looking straight at me, "the reason she's spending the weekend with us is that she's competing in the Junior Chef Cook-Off."

"Oh, that explains the crazy hat," I said. "But I've got to tell you, Judy, you're missing out on one delicious pizza here. We ordered triple cheese with pepperoni."

"No one calls me Judy," she said without cracking a smile. "My full name is Judith Ann. Just like your full name is Henry—which is what I'm going to call you."

"You can do that," I said with my mouth full. "But I won't answer."

Ashley and Frankie burst out laughing, shooting some pretty powerful garlic breath into the air.

"He's been 'Hank' since we were in preschool," Frankie told her.

"He's definitely not a 'Henry' type," Ashley added. "Henrys have gray hair and are math teachers."

"Yeah." I laughed. "I can't even subtract, so you better stick with Hank. Tell me, Judy . . . I mean Judith . . . I mean Judith Ann. What's your favorite thing to cook, aside from weird pizza?"

"Well, for the Junior Chef Cook-Off this weekend, I'll be preparing my special vegetarian meatballs."

"Wait a minute." I stopped eating and scratched my head. "What makes it a meatball if there's no meat? I mean, if there's no meat, then it's just a ball."

Frankie and Ashley cracked up again. Judith Ann was not amused.

"My vegetarian meatballs are made of chopped eggplant, carrots, mushrooms, white beans, and of course, bread crumbs."

"Oh, they sound . . . so . . . um . . . interesting," Ashley said.

"And round," Frankie added.

Judith Ann seemed pleased. "I got the idea from watching my favorite TV show, *Country Cooking for the City*. They were making vegetarian hot dogs."

The idea of a hot dog made of mushed-up cauliflower almost made me gag. So I decided it'd be best to just eat some pepperoni pizza and talk about TV shows.

"Wait a minute—on all of TV, *that's* your favorite show?" I said to Judith Ann, taking a bite of my new slice of pizza. "My favorite is *Zombats*. It's about these really scary zombie bats. You'd love it."

"I don't really like hairy rodents," Judith Ann said. "Besides, I only watch cooking shows on TV."

"Too bad," I said. "Just like this pizza, you're missing out." I tried to offer Judith Ann a slice, one with a juicy piece of pepperoni right in the middle, but she just made a face.

"How about if I make you guys some real food?" Judith Ann said.

"I need to practice for the contest anyway, and you can be my tasters. Maybe my cooking will take your taste buds on a new adventure."

"Oh, that sounds like such fun, doesn't it, kids?" my mom said with a little too much enthusiasm.

"Yeah, it really does," Emily agreed.

"Emily, you have a chore to do first," my dad said. "Katherine's cage needs cleaning. When you have a pet, you have to take care of it."

Cheerio wagged his tail and started chasing it. When he runs in a circle, he looks just like a Cheerio. That's how he got his name.

"Oh, that's right, Daddy," Emily said. Then turning to Judith Ann, she added, "Katherine is my pet iguana. She's really pretty. And she doesn't like a pellet-poop buildup."

For just a second, Judith Ann looked like she was going to throw up. But she recovered in time to squeak out, "I'll be in the kitchen when you're finished."

Ashley and Frankie and I had been planning to watch *The Swamp Monster* for the fortieth time. But before I knew it, my mom had herded us into the kitchen to watch Judith Ann wash her eggplants and carrots and mushrooms.

So long, Swamp Monster. Good-bye, fun.

It was going to be a vegetarian meatball kind of night.

CHAPTER 2

I honestly don't know why everyone was making such a big deal out of Judith Ann. Cooking doesn't seem that hard to me. Even I can cook.

FIVE THINGS I CAN COOK WITH ONE HAND TIED BEHIND MY BACK

BY HANK ZIPZER

1. Toast. (If you're looking for adventure, add grape jelly.)

2. A glass of ice water. (Don't put in too much ice, or the cubes will stick to your lips.)

3. A peanut butter sandwich. (Take small bites, or you'll never open your mouth again.)

4. A s'more. (Make sure you melt the marshmallow really well or it will taste like the inside of a pillow.)

5. Trail mix. (Put a bunch of raisins in a plastic bag. Leave out the nuts and seeds and all the stuff that looks like pebbles. Some people might call this a bag of raisins, but I call it Hank's Perfect Trail Mix.)

CHAPTER 3

Everyone but Emily and my dad gathered in the kitchen, which seemed to make Judith Ann very happy. I could tell she liked being the center of attention. I mean, why else would a person walk around wearing a puffy chef's hat?

First, we had to watch Judith Ann unpack and wash her vegetables. That was about as exciting as watching your toenails grow. She had brought two suitcases. One was for her clothes,

15

and the other was filled to the brim with vegetables.

"You have to treat vegetables gently," she explained, "so they won't bruise."

"Talking about bruises," I blurted out. "You should have seen the one I got last week when we were playing dodgeball."

"You mean when Nick McKelty nailed you in the knee with the ball?" Frankie asked.

"Your whole kneecap turned totally purple," Ashley added.

"Yeah." I laughed. "It looked like Judith Ann's eggplant was growing out of my leg."

I reached out and grabbed her eggplant off the kitchen

counter and held it to my knee.

"See how purple and gross
I am," I said, doing my best
eggplant voice. I had never
talked like an eggplant before,
but I have to say, I did a pretty
good job. I wondered what other
vegetables I could sound like.
A carrot would have a *looooong*
voice. And a cauliflower would
have a *b–b–b–bumpy* voice.

Frankie and Ashley burst out

laughing. My mom didn't. In fact, she gave me that *I don't approve* look.

"Hank, be respectful," she said. "Judith Ann is trying to win a competition, and we need to support her."

Judith Ann took the eggplant from me, put it on our wooden chopping block, and began to cut it into little pieces.

"Henry," she said, "you can help me by peeling the carrots."

"Sorry, Judith Ann," I said. "The only thing I know how to peel is a banana."

She wasn't taking no for an answer. Instead, she took out a vegetable peeler and demonstrated how you scrape it along the carrot to take the skin off.

"All professional cooks have an assistant," she said, handing me the peeler. "I'd like you to be mine."

"Wait a minute! Since when did I become your assistant?"

"Since just now," she said.

I took the peeler and started scraping the carrot. Nothing was happening.

"The peel of the carrot is not

going anywhere,"
I said. "It must
be glued on."

"You're using
the wrong side,"
Ashley whispered. "You have to
use the sharp side."

"I knew that," I said, which of
course I didn't.

Judith Ann spent the next half
hour chopping everything—carrots,
mushrooms, celery, little chunks
of toasted bread. Luckily, she
stopped short of chopping up her
socks. She was chopping so fast
that if my mom hadn't stopped
her, she would have chopped the
kitchen table into little pieces.

"Hey, guys," Frankie whispered

to Ashley and me as Judith Ann started rolling her meatballs. "Who wants  to come with me tomorrow to the hockey game? My dad's got tickets."

"No, thanks," Ashley said. "I'm not a hockey fan. I can never even see that little puck."

"Well, you can count me in," I said. "It sounds great."

I couldn't stop smiling. That is, until I asked my dad if I could go. He had only one word for me. It was a short word. I'll give you a hint. It starts with an **N** and ends with an **O**.

§§ CHAPTER 4

I couldn't believe that my father had said no.

"But, Dad," I wailed. "It's a professional hockey game. And the season is almost over."

"I'm sorry, Hank," he said. "Your cousin has come all the way from Chicago, and she is our guest. Tomorrow's the cook-off, and we are going to support her."

Frankie left for his apartment, and the rest of us stood around watching Judith Ann take the meatballs out of the pot.

"Would you like to taste one, Henry?" she asked me.

"They're actually not bad," Ashley said through her full mouth. "A little squishy, but I could get used to it."

"No offense, Judith Ann," I said. "But I like meatballs that don't squish. You know, ones that leave little chunks of meat between your teeth for later."

"After eating my meatballs, the only thing that will stay in your mouth is the delicious taste," Judith Ann said. "Little chunks left behind aren't part of the fine-food experience."

I had heard enough from Judith

Ann about fine food. My face turned red, and my mouth went out of control.

"Listen," I said, "I know fifty ways to make a great peanut butter sandwich. So don't talk to me about fine food. My taste buds are as good as yours. Maybe even better."

"Peanut butter should never be let out of its jar," Judith Ann said. "It's a snack for three-year-olds."

My mom could tell that I was mad.

"Okay, everyone," she said in her most cheery voice. "I think we should call it a night. We have to get up early tomorrow to get to the cook-off on time."

"The cook-off sounds like fun. Can I go, too?" Ashley asked.

"Of course," my mom said. "We'd love to have you, if it's okay with your parents."

As if the night hadn't been bad enough, it got worse when my mom sprang some surprising news on me: Judith Ann needed somewhere to sleep, and my mom had offered her *my* bed without even asking me.

"But, Mom," I whined. "That's my bed. The mattress is shaped like my body. It looks forward to me every night."

"I've set up your sleeping bag on the floor in Emily's room," my mom said. "It will be just like camping out."

"Yeah, camping out next to a creature who doesn't like me and is going to hiss at me all night long. And I don't mean the iguana."

"Hank, it's only two nights," my mom said. "It will be fine."

At that very moment, the kitchen door burst open, and Emily stuck her head in.

"Mom!" she screamed. "You've got to come quickly. Katherine is spitting up a lettuce ball. It's all green and slimy."

Okay, let me ask you a question. If you had to spend your Friday night cooking meatless meatballs, then sleep on the hard, cold floor of your

know-it-all sister's room with
a barfing iguana spitting lettuce
balls at your face, how would you
feel?

Yup, that's the way I felt,
too.

CHAPTER 5

The Junior Chef Cook-Off
was being held at the Manhattan
Cooking Institute, which is a fancy
school where people go to learn
to be chefs. Since the school is
closed on Saturdays, they let the
junior chefs take over the school's
huge kitchen for the competition.
When we arrived, we were greeted
at the door by a large, round
woman wearing a white jacket
and a hairnet. Her name was
written in red above her pocket.

"Hello, Ms. Smelly," I said, trying so hard to read her name.

"Young man," she answered. "My name is Fern Smiley."

"I'm really glad," I said, "because that's so much better than Smelly."

Ashley quickly covered her mouth, trying to keep in a laugh. I snickered, too. My mom put a firm hand on my shoulder, as if to say, *That will be quite enough out of you.*

"My niece, Judith Ann Zipzer, is part of the cook-off," she said to Ms. Smiley, who by the way, wasn't smiling.

"I've brought my ingredients with me," Judith Ann said.

Ms. Smiley looked down at the suitcase Judith Ann was carrying.

"Very good," she said. "I'm glad to see you've followed our directions."

"Where should I go?" Judith Ann asked. Her voice sounded shaky, like she was nervous. That surprised me. The night before, she had acted so confident, like she was the queen of all cooks.

"What are you waiting for, Junior Chef Zipzer?" Ms. Smiley snapped. "The competition is due to begin in five minutes. Our kitchens run like hands on a clock, perfectly on time. Proceed to kitchen station number seven. Ticktock, young lady."

Judith Ann picked up her suitcase, dashed across the large room to kitchen station number seven, and quickly started unpacking her vegetables. We followed her.

"Junior chefs," Ms. Smiley called out. "Please look on your cutting boards for a printed sheet of our safety rules. You must read it and sign your name, to show that you understand and will follow the rules."

Judith Ann picked up the paper. She had a funny look on her face.

"Henry," she said to me. "Remember, you're my assistant. You have to read me these rules."

I picked up the sheet of paper. The words all floated around on the page, like fish swimming in the ocean.

"I'm not that good at reading," I said to her. "You'll have to read this yourself."

"I don't have time," Judith Ann snapped. "Can't you see I'm preparing my vegetables?"

"I'll get Ashley to help," I said. "She's such a good

reader, she could read this backward, standing on her head, with one eye closed."

Ashley came over and read the rules while Judith Ann set up.

"Fine," Judith Ann said. "I agree to everything. Who has a pen I can use?"

I reached into my backpack to look for a pen, but all I found was my brown-paper-bag lunch. I pulled it out and handed it to Ashley.

"Hold this and don't eat my lunch," I warned her. "I made it myself."

"And that's why I'd never touch it," Ashley said with a laugh.

I found the pen at the bottom of the backpack and handed it to Judith Ann, who signed the paper.

"Okay," she said, "now we're ready to begin."

"We?" I asked.

"Yes, Henry. You're my assistant."

I sighed, handed Ashley my backpack and lunch bag, and took my place next to Judith Ann.

I looked around the room. Eight mini-kitchens were set up. Each one had a stove, an oven, a counter for chopping, and a tiny sink. Stations one through six were already occupied by serious-looking kid chefs. They all looked nervous, but none of them as nervous as Judith Ann.

"Hank," she said, her voice sounding very scared, "when the bell rings for the cook-off to start, we have to be a perfect team. You wash. I chop. The end."

I looked out into the audience and saw Ashley giving me a thumbs-up. I gave her one back.

"Stop clowning around," I heard a stern voice say. "Our chefs are required to have a serious attitude about this competition."

I spun around to see Ms. Smiley squinting at me over the top of her glasses. "Oh," I said. "I'm not one of the chefs. I'm just a vegetable washer."

"He's my assistant," Judith Ann explained. "And it won't happen again."

"No, it won't," Ms. Smiley said, "because assistants are not allowed in this contest. Each chef must do his or her own work, start to finish."

"Tough luck," I said to Judith Ann as I started walking away. "I wish I could stay, but rules are rules." Then, turning to Ms. Smiley, I added, "I'm not really the assistant type, anyway.

In my kitchen, I'm the main guy."

Before she could answer, Ms. Smiley's pocket started to ring. Or at least, the phone in her pocket started to ring.

"Chef Smiley here," she said, putting the phone to her ear. She listened for a minute, and then said, "You can't make it for even an hour? Okay, I have no choice but to understand." She put the phone back in her jacket pocket and shook her head.

"This is terrible news," she said to us. "One of our junior chefs just called in sick."

"I hope he didn't get sick from eating his own cooking," I joked.

Ms. Smiley ignored me. "This is unacceptable," she said. "We have announced that there are eight contestants. That's what we promised!"

She straightened her hairnet and looked like she was about to panic. Then suddenly, her expression changed. I'm not going to say she looked happy, but at least she didn't look like she was going to explode.

Ms. Smiley laid a beefy hand on my shoulder.

"Perhaps I could use you," she said.

"Use me to do what?"

"I heard you say that in your kitchen you're the main guy."

"You heard correctly," I said, puffing my chest out.

"Excellent. You will take station six. We need all stations full for the photographs."

Photographs. I liked the sound of that.

"The photos will run in all the New York newspapers," she said. "The cook-off is receiving great attention, because our grand prize is so special."

"Really? What does the winner get?" I asked.

"The grand prize is a television appearance on *Country Cooking for the City*," explained Judith Ann, who had been listening to our whole conversation. "But you don't have to concern yourself with that, Henry, since I am going to win."

I've never been on TV, but deep down, I always felt I should be. All I would have to do is flash a little of the old Zipzer attitude, and *boom*, I'd have my own TV show. To be honest, I couldn't resist the idea.

"I'm your guy," I said to Ms. Smiley. "You can call me Mr. Station Number Six."

"But, Henry," Judith Ann said, "you can't cook. And even if you could, you have no food."

"Don't worry, young man," Ms. Smiley said. "There is already food at station number six. The contestant sent it in advance."

"I hope it's something I know how to cook," I said.

"Of course it is," Ms. Smiley answered. "It's quite a simple dish. Artichokes stuffed with crab legs and capers."

"No problem," I said.

Okay, truth time. I had no idea what an artichoke was, and I had never even heard the word *caper*. As for crab legs,

all I could do was hope the crab
wasn't going to pinch me.

"Are you ready to
participate?" Ms. Smiley said.

"You bet!" I exclaimed with
a big smile.

That's what my face and mouth
said. But the rest of my body
was screaming, "*Hank* . . . .
*nooooooooooo! What did you get
yourself into?*"

CHAPTER 6

THREE WAYS I COULD GET OUT OF THIS MESS
BY HANK ZIPZER

1. I could put on big floppy clown shoes and do a crazy clown dance. (Wait a minute, I forgot my clown shoes at home. Wait a minute, I don't have clown shoes. Never did.)

2. I could run outside and get a taxi and ask the driver to take me to the North Pole. (Wait a minute, I don't have any money. Wait a minute, I do have a nickel stuck to a gummy bear at the bottom of my backpack.)

3. I could run over to my mom, throw on my jacket, grab my lunch bag, and run for it. (Wait a minute . . . my lunch bag. Did you hear what I just said? My lunch bag! YES! That's the answer.)

CHAPTER 7

To be truthful, my lunch bag wasn't entirely the answer. It was only half an answer. The contest was starting in less than a minute. Ms. Smiley hurried me over to station number six.

"Your ingredients are laid out on the cutting board," she said to me. "There will be two judges. Do the best you can. Just make sure you look busy for the photographers."

With that, she disappeared into the big kitchen space and

left me staring at the cutting board in front of me.

There were a couple of crab legs still inside their shells. I thought I saw them wiggle. There was a jar of little green raisin-type things in juice. I figured those were the capers. And right in the middle of the cutting board were some baseball-size green things that looked like cactuses. They had a whole lot of leaves, and each leaf had a sharp thorn at the end of it. I know this because when I picked one up, it felt like a needle had pricked my finger.

"Ow!" I screamed.

Judith Ann looked up at me from her station.

"That happened to me the first time I picked up an artichoke," she said. "Those things should come with a warning sign."

"And a pair of gloves," I added. "There's no way I can make anything out of this. It's dangerous."

"You have to cook something," Judith Ann said. "You don't want to look bad in front of the photographers."

"Never fear, Hank is here," I said. "With a plan. Actually, half a plan."

I bolted from my station.

I grabbed my lunch bag from Ashley. I knew exactly what was in there, because I had made it myself. A peanut butter and grape jelly sandwich, with some extra strawberry jam thrown in for fun. A banana with no brown spots. A box of chocolate milk with a straw. A plastic bag with a chocolate chip cookie and an oatmeal raisin cookie, because I didn't want my tongue to get bored. And a *Happy Birthday* napkin left over from Emily's reptile birthday party.

"What are you doing, Hank?" Ashley asked.

There was no time to answer. I made it back to my station with my lunch bag just as the starting bell rang. Ms. Smiley's voice came over the loudspeaker.

"Attention, junior chefs," she announced. "You have forty-five minutes to create your favorite dish. After that, our judges will perform a taste test and select our two finalists. You cannot look at a written recipe. You cannot pick your nose, touch your hair, or otherwise dirty your fingers. You cannot borrow another contestant's food. Now—ready, set, cook!"

The first thing I did was push

the artichoke and crab legs off
the cutting board, being careful
not to get pricked again. Then
I put my brown paper bag right
in the center of the board.

I looked around at the other
kitchen stations. The chefs were
hard at work. In one station, a
curly-haired girl wearing goggles
was chopping tomatoes. Boy,
were they juicy. It's a good
thing she had on those goggles,
because the tomato seeds were
squirting all over her face.

Next to her, a teenage boy
with green streaks in his hair
was chopping onions. He was
crying like a baby. He could have
used that other girl's goggles.

Right next to Judith Ann was
a girl named Lily Chun who's in
the fifth grade at my school.
I know because her class comes
to help us during language arts,
and she tutored me in spelling.
She was really nice when I
couldn't remember how to spell
any of my words except for
"cat." I could tell Lily was going
to bake a cake, because she
was pouring flour into a bowl. It
looked like she was in the middle

of a white dust storm. There was
flour everywhere—on her hands, on
her apron, even on her nose.

"Hank!" a voice called from
the audience. It was Ashley.
"Get going. Do something.
You've been just standing there
for ten minutes."

"Oh, right," I said. I could feel my mind coming back to earth. Sometimes it wanders far away without even asking permission. I want to concentrate on what's happening in front of me, but my mind has ideas of its own.

I looked around and saw Ms. Smiley walking up and down between the kitchen stations. She was loudly slurping an iced coffee through a straw.

"Where is the artichoke?" she asked me. *Slurp, slurp, slurp.*

"I rejected it to protect my nine other fingertips. But don't worry, I have something else to cook."

She nodded and walked away.

"You'd better hurry up," Judith Ann whispered. "I already have all my mushrooms scrubbed and chopped."

I picked up my lunch bag, turned it upside down, and let everything fall onto the counter.

I took my sandwich out of the plastic bag. Okay, that was something. I was on the road; I just didn't know where it was going.

I looked around and saw that everyone was chopping something. So I picked up a knife and chopped my sandwich into little bits. I did the same thing with the banana. I'm not very good with a knife, so I chopped slowly to make sure my fingers stayed on my hand.

Then I took out the cookies. I took a bite of the chocolate chip one.

Hank, stop eating your ingredients, I told myself. *Otherwise, your entire project is going to be inside your stomach.*

I chopped the cookies into little pieces, and then stood back and thought about the pile of food in front of me. I wish I could tell you that I had a bright idea about what to do with it. But I didn't, and time was running out.

My eyes darted around the room, searching for an idea. All I saw was a bunch of kids hard at work, and Ms. Smiley pacing around with her iced coffee. *Slurp, slurp, slurp.*

There it is! I thought. *Slurp, slurp, slurp.*

The answer to what I was going to make was right in front of me.

CHAPTER 8

I stuck my hand in the air and waved it around wildly, trying to get Ms. Smiley's attention. At last, she noticed and came stomping over to me.

"What is it now, young man?" she asked.

"Do you have a blender I can use?" I asked.

"There is a blender on the counter right in front of you," she snapped.

"Oh, right," I said.

"Sometimes I can't do two things at once—like think and look."

"I suggest you concentrate," she said. "You're wasting precious time."

She was right. I noticed that Judith Ann was already putting her meatballs into the pot.

I scooped up all the pieces of my chopped lunch and carefully dropped them into the blender jar. Then I pulled the straw from the carton of chocolate milk and poked it inside. Turning the carton upside down, I squeezed it and watched the milk squirt into the blender through the straw. I made sure I got every last drop out of the carton.

"It's showtime!" I called to Judith Ann.

With a big grin, I pushed the blender's start button. *Oops!* I had forgotten to put the top on. Chocolate milk and bananas and cookies and chunks of sandwich flew out the top of the blender and landed smack in the middle of my face. A few chunks sprayed on Judith Ann's counter.

"Henry!" she cried. "Turn off the blender and put the top on. Don't get your mess on my meatballs!"

I switched off the blender and put as much of the goop as I could back inside.

"Six-minute warning," Ms. Smiley called over the loudspeaker.

I put the top back on the blender and turned it on. At least everything stayed inside this time. I stood there watching my lunch swirl around in the blender jar. The banana, the peanut butter and jelly sandwich, and the cookies turned to liquid, blending with the chocolate milk to make a thick, frothy smoothie.

"Look at that," I said, pointing to the glass jar of the blender. "It's a work of art."

"It's a mess," Judith Ann said. "Fine cooking is not throwing things into a blender and hoping for the best."

"I'm not *hoping* for the best," I snapped back. "It *is* the best."

Truthfully, I had no idea what my smoothie was going to taste like. It did turn a pretty ugly shade of mud brown, not a color that makes your taste buds stand up and say hello.

I poured my smoothie into two glasses, one for each judge, and put each glass on its own little plate.

"Psst, Hank," I heard Ashley

call from the audience. "I watch cooking shows on TV all the time. The winners always make their dish look pretty. You need to dress those plates up."

The only thing I could think of was the half-eaten box of gummy bears in my backpack. I left my station and ran to get it. Of course, it wasn't where I thought I had put it. I had to unzip every little pocket until I found it buried beneath my crumpled-up spelling test. (By the way, I got a D-minus, which is better than an F.)

When I returned to the counter, I emptied the box into my hand and spread the colorful gummy bears around the edge of the plates.

Ashley was right. All of a sudden, my smoothies looked like a party on a plate. Now all I had to do was wait for the judges.

When the buzzer rang, the two judges appeared.

"Our first judge is Maxine Nosebomb, the head pastry chef at Café Sweetooth," Ms. Smiley announced. Ms. Nosebomb waved her hand at us.

"Our other judge," Ms. Smiley continued, "is Bob Bones, master chef of one of our city's finest restaurants, Robert's Kitchen."

He looked like he was going
to be a strict judge.

I stood at my station while
the two judges went down the
row, starting at kitchen station
number one. They stopped and
chatted with each junior chef,
including Goggle Girl and Crying
Onion Boy. At each chef's
station, the judges took one
bite of the dish and made notes
on their clipboards. When they

got to Judith Ann, I could see that her hands were shaking. She tried to smile, but her lips were quivering so much, it looked like they were doing the Chicken Dance.

"It's my pleasure to invite you to taste my special meatless meatballs," she told the judges.

I could tell she had been practicing that sentence all the way from Chicago.

Chef Bones and Chef Nosebomb each popped a meatball into their mouths. I waited for them to scream in horror, but just the opposite happened. Ms. Nosebomb actually made a purring sound like a kitty cat. I saw Bob Bones wiggle his mustache. I wasn't sure if that was a good or bad sign.

Then the judges turned to me.

"What have we here?" Ms. Nosebomb asked.

"An entire lunch in a glass," I said proudly. "I call it Hank's Peanut Butter and Jelly Smoothie with Surprise Ingredients."

From her station, I heard Judith Ann let out a big sigh. The judges were supposed to take only one sip of my smoothie. But after that sip, they took another and another, until they each finished their entire glass! Chef Bones

even licked his mustache clean
because he didn't want to miss
a drop. I could see Ashley out in
the audience, clapping her hands.

The two judges walked off
with Ms. Smiley, and I saw them
all whispering in the corner. I
was surprised at how nervous
I had suddenly become. My
stomach went from calm to crazy
in a matter of seconds.

"The judges have selected the

two finalists," Ms. Smiley said. "They will compete against each other in tomorrow's final cook-off, which will take place on the set of *Country Cooking for the City*."

The room became silent, as everyone in the audience moved to the edge of their chairs.

"Finalist number one," Maxine Nosebomb declared, "is Judith Ann Zipzer, who impressed us with her delicious meatless meatballs."

Judith Ann started to squeal, and then slapped her hand over her mouth to stop the sound. What came out sounded more like a burp.

"Our second finalist," Bob Bones announced, "has produced a creative and original sweet delight."

I glanced over at Lily Chun, whose entire head of hair had turned white from the flour she used to make her cake. She was looking pretty confident, and she had every reason to be. Her cake was beautiful and decorated with flower petals.

"And the second winning chef is . . ."

Lily stepped forward, ready to receive her award.

"Hank Zipzer, for his unique and yummy Peanut Butter and Jelly Smoothie with Surprise Ingredients."

I couldn't believe my ears.
I threw my arms in the air, jumped
as high as my short legs would
take me, and hollered, "Let's hear
it for me!" Ashley screamed my
name. And my mom was hopping
around in a circle.

Before I knew it, a photographer
was pulling Judith Ann and me
out from behind our stations and
snapping our picture. The other
junior chefs came to shake our
hands, even Lily Chun.

"Isn't this great?" I said to Judith Ann. "We're in the finals. Now we can be cousins *and* friends."

She didn't answer. She just turned and walked out of the room. I could tell she was upset, but I didn't know why. I mean, the judges liked her meatballs, but they probably thought my smoothie was more fun.

Hey, it's not my fault you can't drink a meatball through a straw.

CHAPTER 9

There are only two words that could describe the mood in our apartment that night: Dark gray cloud. Okay, that's three words, but you get the idea.

The dark gray cloud, also known as Judith Ann Zipzer, was in a major bad mood. From the way she was acting, you would have thought she had lost the cooking competition.

"Cheer up, Judy," I said to her as she sat at the kitchen

table polishing her vegetables. "You're one of the two finalists."

"First of all, Henry," she snapped, "it's not Judy, it's Judith Ann. We've gone over that before. And second of all, my victory means nothing when the other finalist is you—and your peanut butter mess."

Ouch. That girl had one sharp tongue.

I was never so glad to hear the doorbell ring. I raced out of the kitchen with my ears still burning.

It was my grandfather, Papa Pete, at the door. He was wearing the red running suit he always wears on the weekends.

Comfort first is his motto. Papa Pete's face was so happy that the mood in the house changed immediately.

"Hey, Hankie," he shouted as he came in the door. "Give your grandpa a big hug."

Papa Pete is so tall that when he hugs you, he lifts you right off your feet.

"I hear you're a champion cook," he said. "Just like me."

Papa Pete ran the Crunchy Pickle, which is a deli on Broadway, a block away from our apartment. My mom runs it now. She's into health food and is trying to make luncheon meats good for you. Her specialty is soylami—which is a combination of gray soy stuff and other non-salami type things. It's got everything in it but taste. Papa Pete still works at the sandwich counter at lunchtime and slips real salami into the sandwiches. You always know when someone's eating a Papa Pete sandwich because they're smiling while they're chewing.

"Papa Pete, you won't believe what I did," I told him. "My winning dish came to me in a flash."

"Your mother told me," he said

with a grin. "Lunch in a glass. I love the sound of that."

"And if it wins, I could become really famous. First, I'll demonstrate it on TV. And then, every restaurant in New York will have it on the menu. We could even put a sign in front of the Crunchy Pickle that says 'Home of Hank Zipzer's Famous Lunch in a Glass.' We'll have lines around the block. We'll have to hire our own security guard."

"Slow down there, Hankie," Papa Pete said. "You haven't won yet."

"Don't tell Judith Ann," I whispered in his ear, "but I really hope I do!"

"It'll be our secret," he whispered back. We hooked our pinkie fingers together then pulled them apart. It was our code for keeping a secret.

Holding up a brown paper bag he had brought, Papa Pete said a loud voice, "Attention, Zipzer family. I brought dinner. Pickles, potato salad, and sandwiches. Half pastrami, half soylami."

"And guess which ones are going to be left over," I said.

"I like soylami," Emily said, coming into the room wearing her iguana around her neck like a scarf.

"That's because all five of your taste buds are asleep on your tongue," I said.

"For your information, the human tongue has between two thousand and eight thousand taste buds," Emily said. "And all of mine are wide awake, thank you very much."

"Really? Because I thought I heard them snoring."

Papa Pete let out one of his great big laughs, the kind that make his whole body shake.

"Don't encourage him, Pete," my father said, looking up from his crossword puzzle. "Reward Hank when his grades improve, not for his wisecracks."

Papa Pete and my mom took the sandwiches and pickles out of the bag.

"Come have dinner with us," my mom called to Judith Ann. "We have a delicious deli sandwich waiting for you."

The kitchen door swung open, and Judith Ann stuck her head out.

"Congratulations to you!" Papa Pete said to her, reaching

out to shake her hand. "I heard you wowed the judges, too. I love a good meatball myself. My secret is lots of garlic. What's yours?"

"No meat," she told him.

"Oh," Papa Pete said. "I never would have thought of that. Meatless, huh? So I bet you'll pick one of these soylami sandwiches, right?"

"I can't join you for dinner," Judith Ann said. "I have to practice making my dish one more time. Everything has to be perfect for the finals tomorrow."

Miss Dark Gray Cloud disappeared back into the kitchen.

"She's a serious young woman," Papa Pete said. "Okay, who wants soylami?"

"Me!" Emily shouted.

"Not me!" I shouted. "I'll take the real pastrami. And lots of mustard."

"Oh, mustard!" Papa Pete said. "I knew I forgot something."

"That's all right." I hopped to my feet. "I'll get it."

As I walked into the kitchen, I expected to see piles of vegetables all over the kitchen counter, and Judith Ann chopping up a storm. But that isn't what I saw at all.

What I saw was something I never thought I'd see in my whole life.

Judith Ann was crying. And by crying, I don't mean a few tears. She had turned herself into a

major waterworks factory. She
was sitting on the floor with
her head in her hands, the tears
squirting out of her eyes like she
was a lawn sprinkler.

"Judith Ann?" I said. "Did
you cut yourself when you were
chopping your vegetables?"

She shook her head no.

"Did you fall down?"

Again, she shook her head no.

"Well, were you attacked by one of your eggplants?"

I thought that would make her laugh, but it didn't. In fact, she cried even louder.

I didn't know what I was supposed to do, so I just sat down next to her on the floor. I pulled a dish towel off the oven door handle and handed it to her. We just sat there for a minute, while she wiped her tears in the dish towel.

"I think I know what it is," I said at last. "You're homesick. Boy, do I know how that feels. My school had a sleepover at the beach for one night. Don't tell anyone, but I spent the whole night crying into my sleeping bag."

"That's not it," Judith Ann said. "I'm not homesick. I'm scared."

I looked around our kitchen to see what was so scary. I didn't see anything except regular kitchen stuff.

"Are you scared of the refrigerator?" I asked. "It's tall, but it doesn't bite."

"You don't understand how much I need to win this contest," Judith Ann said. "I told everyone at my school I was going to win. I even told my principal, Mrs. Denney! And I'm afraid I might not. That's what I'm scared of."

"Look at it this way, Judy.

You're going to come in first or second. Either way, that's not bad."

"I need to come in first."

"Why? What's the big deal?"

"I'm going to tell you a secret, Hank. Cooking is the only thing I'm really good at."

"But you're so smart and confident and everything," I told her. "It seems like you can do anything."

"I'm terrible in school," she said. "Reading is really hard for me, and I can't spell either."

"Welcome to the club," I almost shouted. "When my teacher tells me to sound out a word, I have no idea what she's talking about. The only sound I hear is my brain skidding to a stop."

I stuck my hand out to shake hers, but she didn't take it.

"My parents are always telling me that if I just try harder, I'll get it," she said in a voice that sounded really sad. "But no matter how hard I try, I still get bad grades. When I discovered cooking, it was the first time I felt like I was really good at something. I've won every contest I've been in, but this is the big one. If I win, it would make my parents so proud."

"I've been trying to make my dad proud since I was a baby," I said. "And I always come up a little short—which stinks, because I am short to begin with."

Judith Ann actually laughed a little. That made me feel better for her, until I realized that my "lunch in a glass" was going to be a big problem for her. Way down deep, I knew it was a winner.

"Listen, Judith Ann," I said, getting up. "Why don't you just relax and have a sandwich with us? You don't need to practice. You're already a great cook."

"I wish I could be relaxed like you," she said. "But I have to make the recipe one more time. Just to be extra sure. You go have a sandwich. I'm going to stay here."

As I walked back through the swinging door into the dining room, I thought about Judith Ann. Papa Pete always says, "You can't judge a book by its cover." I never understood until now. On the outside, Judith Ann acted like she was the queen of the world. But on the inside, she was just

like me—all shaky, like a bowl of
Jell-O.

"There he is," Papa Pete said
as I took a seat at the table.
"One pastrami sandwich, and one
dill pickle, coming right up."

"You forgot to bring the
mustard," Emily pointed out.

"Hank would forget his head
if it wasn't attached to his neck,"
my dad said with a snort.

"You're going to do so well
tomorrow, honey," my mom said.

She always tries to say something nice after my dad says something mean.

"He's going to knock their socks off," Papa Pete said. "And make me a promise, Hankie. When they pick you to be on *Country Cooking for the City*, you be sure to make me your assistant. Everyone on television has an assistant. Boy oh boy, the guys on my bowling team are going to be so impressed. I'll have to give autographs at the bowling alley."

Papa Pete let out one of his big laughs. I could tell he loved the idea of being on TV.

So did I.

But the problem was, so did Judith Ann.

CHAPTER 10

"Is this the TV station?" I asked my mom the next morning as we turned into a revolving door in a big glass building.

"This is the address they gave me," my mom said.

My mom, dad, and Papa Pete were there, along with Frankie and Ashley, and of course, Judith Ann. All of us walked into the huge lobby with big couches and hundreds of TV screens all over the walls.

The guard took us to the elevators.

"What floor?" my dad asked.

"Thirty-five," the guard answered, pushing the button. "That's where it all happens."

And boy was he right. When the doors opened, we stepped out and immediately found ourselves smack in the middle of the *Country Cooking for the City* set.

"Wow," said Papa Pete. "It looks so much bigger on TV."

"Dude," Frankie whispered to me. "This is awesome."

"Hank, look!" Ashley said. "There's the kitchen where the chefs work. And there are the cameras. Aren't you nervous?"

I wasn't nervous. I was proud to be there. I was proud that my friends and family would be there to see me win.

"This could be the best day of my life," I told Frankie. "It ranks right up there with that time Dad and I won the three-legged race at the Root Beer Bust at school. Remember that, Dad?"

"I remember I ripped my pants

and had to spend fourteen dollars to get them fixed," he answered.

"Oh my gosh," Ashley said, grabbing my arm. "OH MY GOSH. Look who's coming to get us."

Walking across the studio to us was Chuck Hall, the host of *Country Cooking for the City*. He was tall, with a huge head of blond hair, and teeth as white as marshmallows. When she saw him, Judith Ann actually let out a shriek. She stepped forward and stuck out her hand.

"What an honor to meet you," she said to Chuck. "I've never missed one of your shows."

Chuck smiled. I could tell he was expecting the rest of us to chime in, too. To be honest, I had never seen one of his shows, but I knew better than to say that out loud.

"So," Chuck said to Judith Ann, "I assume you're one of my finalists. Who's the other one?"

"He's your guy," Frankie told Chuck, pointing to me. "Hank Zipzer."

"Nice to meet you, Mr. Zipper," Chuck said with a marshmallow grin.

"It's Zipzer," I said. "And by

the way, do you know what has
a hundred and thirty-seven teeth
and no cavities? A zipper!"

Everyone laughed but Chuck.

"If you don't mind, son, I'll do
the jokes," he said. "Now follow
me, and we'll get you kids set up."

My family and friends got to sit
in the audience seats. Judith Ann
and I were led over to the kitchen
counter, which was in front of the
cameras. Ms. Smiley was there,
setting up the kitchen tools on
the counter.

"I have your blender, young man," she said.

"Thank you, Ms. S.," I said. I would have called her Ms. Smiley, but I was afraid that *Smelly* would come out of my mouth by accident.

"And Judith Ann," she went on, "I have your mixing bowls and skillet. Both of you may begin placing your food supplies on the counter."

I reached into my paper bag and took out the peanut butter and jelly sandwich, the cookies, the milk, and the banana. Way down at the bottom I was surprised to see a pickle and half of a pastrami sandwich in a plastic bag. I knew Papa Pete had snuck that in, in case I got hungry. That's what I love about Papa Pete.

"Are we going to be on TV?" I asked Chuck's assistant, who was walking by with a clipboard.

"The winner of this match is," she said, without looking up.

"Cool. What does the loser get?"

"A hearty handshake," she said with a laugh.

I didn't think that was funny at all.

All of a sudden, the lights in the studio went down, and two bright lights lit Judith Ann and me up.

Chuck walked out and said, "Ladies and gentlemen, please help me welcome our two finalists for the title of Junior Chef Champion."

There were seven people in the audience. Six were my family and friends, and one was the guard who brought us up in the elevator. But when they all clapped for us, it sounded like there were at least ten people.

Chuck looked over at us and spoke in almost a whisper.

"This is your big moment, kids. Are you ready?"

I nodded. Judith Ann gulped. I wished I could have given her some of my confidence.

"Then it's showtime," Chuck said, in his big show-business voice.

And just like that, the contest was on.

CHAPTER 11

We had exactly forty-five minutes to complete our dishes. Judith Ann got right to work. As she chopped her vegetables, I could see sweat forming on her forehead.

"Maybe you should take it easy on that poor little eggplant," I whispered to her. "I thought I just heard it screaming."

"This is no time for jokes," she said. "As I told you, this means everything to me."

I hadn't forgotten that. I was just trying to help her relax.

I knew it wasn't going to take the whole time to make my Peanut Butter and Jelly Smoothie with Surprise Ingredients. But I wanted to look busy, so I took my time tearing the peanut butter and jelly sandwich into bite-size bits. That took about ten seconds, so I tried to go even slower with the banana. After I peeled it one tiny section at a time, I waved to Frankie and Ashley sitting in the audience. They waved back with big smiles.

Judith Ann had finished the vegetables and was rolling them into three plump meatless meatballs.

"Look at you go, Judy," I said. "Those meatballs look really round."

She glanced up at me like she was going to say something. Just then, one of the meatballs she was working on rolled out of her hand and onto the floor.

"Oh no!" she screamed. "Look what you made me do!"

"I didn't mean for that to happen. Honest."

"I know, Hank. It wasn't your fault. I'm just so nervous."

I turned back to my blender and started to crumble the cookies into the jar. Judith Ann put her two meatballs into the frying pan and rolled them around with a wooden spoon. Suddenly, I heard her shout.

"Oh no! What is wrong with me today?" she said. "My meatball is crumbling."

I looked over into her frying pan and saw that one of the meatballs had come apart. It looked like a vegetable pancake.

"I am such a loser," she went on, sounding like she was going to cry. "I practice and I practice, and I can't do anything right."

"Hey, do I ever know that feeling," I said. "I practice my spelling words all night long, and when I get to class, I have no idea where they are. They're sure not in my head."

"I wish I were making

your Peanut Butter and Jelly Smoothie," she said. "It seems so easy."

She definitely had a point. She was chopping and rolling and frying and doing all kinds of complicated cooking stuff. All I was doing was filling a blender and flipping a switch.

As I reached into my bag to get the carton of chocolate milk, I smelled the pickle at the bottom. I looked over at Judith Ann. She was concentrating very hard on her last meatball, rolling it around to make sure it was fully cooked.

It was then that I knew what I had to do.

I reached into my bag and

pulled out Papa Pete's dill pickle. When no one was watching, I dropped it into the blender and put on the top. Then I flipped the switch.

I smiled to myself. Hank's Peanut Butter and Jelly Smoothie with Surprise Ingredients was sure going to have one big surprise ingredient now.

By the time the forty-five minutes were up, I had poured my smoothie into a glass and decorated it with the gummy bears I brought with me in my pocket. Then I popped in a red-and-white-striped straw. Judith Ann had placed her one lonely meatball on top of the pancake one, and dripped some red sauce over both of them. It actually looked pretty good. She had turned her mistake into her own surprise.

Chuck Hall picked up his microphone and stood between us.

"Ladies and gentlemen," he said to the same seven people in the audience. "The Junior Chef Cook-Off is now over, and all that's left to do is the tasting. I'm going to take one taste of each dish, and decide who will appear with me on *Country Cooking for the City*."

Chuck picked up Judith Ann's plate, took a big sniff, then popped a bite of the meatball into his mouth.

"Mmmm . . . very tasty," he said. "And I love the creative way you designed your plate. A meatless meatball on a meatless pancake. So creative."

Then he turned to me, picked up the glass, and smiled.

"This looks yummy," he said. "I love a good smoothie."

He raised the glass to his lips and took a big sip through the straw. I waited, but not for long. He spit the smoothie out of his mouth like he was a fire truck hose.

"What did you put in there?" he gasped. "It's so sour!"

"That was my special ingredient," I explained with my old Zipzer attitude. "I thought it would give my smoothie a personality."

Chuck took a paper napkin and wiped his tongue to try to get the taste out of his mouth. It was pretty clear that he didn't think peanut butter and pickles was a good combo.

"This is the easiest contest I've ever judged," he said, still spitting into the microphone. "The winner, and the contestant who will appear on television, is Judy Zipzer."

"Excuse me, sir," I whispered to him. "She really likes it if you call her Judith Ann."

Judith Ann was the happiest person I had ever seen in my whole life.

In the middle of her happy dance, she suddenly stopped and turned to me.

"I'm so sorry, Hank," she said.

"I'm not," I answered. "You deserved to win. Besides, I still get my hearty handshake from Chuck Hall."

Ashley and Frankie had run down from the audience to be with me.

"We were sure you were going to win," Ashley said.

"Yeah, what happened, Hankster?" Frankie asked.

I just shrugged. My secret ingredient was going to stay my secret forever.

CHAPTER 12

A POP QUIZ
BY HANK ZIPZER

Judith Ann got to demonstrate her meatless meatballs on Country Cooking for the City. Your job on this quiz is to pick the one thing that REALLY happened.

A) She dropped her whole bowl of chopped vegetables all over Chuck Hall's shoes.

B) She thanked me and told the whole world that I, Hank Zipzer, gave her the confidence to win.

C) When she was accepting her award, she opened her mouth to say thank you but a burp came out instead.

ANSWER: The answer is B. Judith Ann gave me the biggest shout-out I've ever gotten in my whole life. So I guess you can say I won, too.